THE DANGEROUS SNAKE AND REPTILE CLUB

BILLY

VICE PRESIDENT

BOBBY

PRESIDENT

MIKE

TREASURER

CRAIG

SCOUT

DANNY

SNAKE TRAINER

MOLLY

GUARD DOG

ANDY

CAPTAIN

Daniel San Souci

TRICYCLE PRESS
Berkeley / Toronto

A Clubhouse Book

AUTHOR'S NOTE

The school children I have talked with over the years are always interested to hear that my brother Robert and I have published many children's books together. They also love listening to stories about the adventures we had growing up in San Francisco and Berkeley, California. We feel that our childhood was magical and was what inspired us to create books. Here is one of our favorite stories. While now we know not to handle wild creatures, Robert and I get a lot of laughs when we tell about the time we started The Dangerous Snake and Reptile Club.

Copyright © 2004 by Daniel San Souci

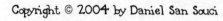 Tricycle Press
a little division of Ten Speed Press
P.O. Box 7123
Berkeley, California 94707
www.tenspeed.com

Design by Toni Tajima and Daniel San Souci
Typeset in Stinky Butt

Library of Congress Cataloging-in-Publication Data
San Souci, Daniel.
  The Dangerous Snake and Reptile Club / by Daniel San Souci.
    p. cm. — (A clubhouse book)
  Summary: Danny, Robert, Mike, and their friends form a club collect and display a dinosaur bone, tadpoles, and a king snake that the brothers found on vacation, as well as creatures from their neighborhood.
  ISBN 1-58246-131-7
  [1. Reptiles—Fiction. 2. Clubs—Fiction. 3. Brothers—Fiction.] I. Title.
  PZ7.S1946Dan 2004
  [Fic]—dc22   2004001176

First Tricycle Press printing, 2004
Printed in Singapore

1 2 3 4 5 6 – 08 07 06 05 04

For Loretta—still the cutest girl in town!

We closed up the clubhouse, said good-bye to our friends and headed off on our family vacation.

Lake County

The ride in the Shipwreck was a long one.

When we arrived in Lake County,
my older brother Bobby found a dinosaur bone under
the old bridge.

Dad said it was probably a beef bone, but Bobby was *sure*
that it had come from a tyrannosaurus rex.

My younger brother Mike was soon standing in the creek, catching tadpoles and putting them in a big pickle jar. He figured that he could sell each for a quarter when they turned into frogs.

I found a king snake on the gravel road. I held it for a while and it didn't seem afraid of me, so I took it back to the cabin.

The vacation days passed quickly.

Mike's pickle jar was full of tadpoles, so he helped Bobby look for more dinosaur bones.

Bobby asked me to help too, but I said "no" because I was having so much fun.

I was the most popular kid around. Nobody called me Danny anymore. I was "the kid with the snake."

The time had come to leave Lake County and head for home.

Bobby tried to convince Dad to stay longer so he could continue to hunt for dinosaur bones. He didn't get very far.

"I hope you're not planning on taking that snake
home with you," Mom said to me. But before I could
answer, Baby Ellen started screaming.

Mom looked over at Dad, who was looking at his watch.
"It's fine with me," he said. "Everyone just get in the car!"

As the Shipwreck pulled up to our house, our friends were there to greet us.

We jumped out of the car.

Craig, Billy, and Andy couldn't believe their eyes when they saw the treasures we had brought home.

The next day we started a new club.

Andy and I drew a picture of a tyrannosaurus rex, showing where the bone had come from.

Bobby and Craig built shelves for the bone, the snake, and the tadpoles.

Mike and Billy painted a huge sign.

We gave the clubhouse

Every day we'd go to the park and search for new creatures to add to our collection.

Soon all the shelves were full of newts, frogs, salamanders, garter snakes, and small lizards.

Mike came up with a great idea. "I bet we could charge a dime to see the inside of the clubhouse."

"The kid around the corner is telling everyone that we have a giant snake from Africa," said Billy. "I know because his mom got mad and called mine. Who wouldn't want to see a giant snake?"

On Saturday we placed a sign on the front lawn that read: "See dangerous snakes, reptiles, and a real dinosaur bone. ONLY 10¢."

In no time at all we had a line of kids and even some parents.

Mike and Craig sold tickets.

Andy and Billy hid with me behind the clubhouse and made jungle noises.

Bobby gave a tour of the Dangerous Snake and Reptile Club.

When he picked up the King snake he asked,
"Does anyone want to hold it?"

At the end of the day we made almost $2.00!

At night I kept the snake under my bed for safekeeping.

One morning I woke up and the snake was gone!

I searched every room and couldn't find it. Mom was having some friends over for lunch, so she was airing out the house. I guessed the snake must have slipped outside.

I quickly rounded up the guys. We spent the entire
morning trying to find the snake.

We finally gave up and figured it was long gone.

A short time after Mom's friends showed up for lunch,
we heard a loud scream coming from the house.

I ran through the back door and into the living room.
Sure enough, someone had found the snake.

I grabbed the snake and ran past Mom, who was coming from the kitchen.

The guys were waiting outside.

"Did anyone throw up?" asked Billy.

"Or get dizzy?" asked Mike.

"Or faint?" asked Andy.

"Or go crazy?" asked Bobby.

"Nope," I said. "They just screamed."

I put the snake back in the clubhouse.

After what had happened, I knew that the snake would be a lot happier if I set it free. At dinner I told the family of my decision.

"That's the right thing to do," said my dad.

The next morning I took the snake to the park and said "good-bye." I felt sad, but if I ever wanted to see it again, I was sure I could find it. After all, we were friends.

The next day Professor Stern's wiener dog got loose,

We chased him,

snuck into the clubhouse, and stole the dinosaur bone.

but he outran us.

It wasn't long afterwards that we let all the newts, salamanders, and other creatures go and ended the Dangerous Snake and Reptile Club.

Then we found a meteor in Mrs. Gray's backyard
and we turned the clubhouse into Space Station Mars.